P9-DYE-923

Santa ~~Claus~~ Bruce

RYAN T. HIGGINS

DISNEY · HYPERION
Los Angeles   New York

For Joanna

Copyright © 2018 by Ryan T. Higgins
All rights reserved. Published by Disney • Hyperion, an imprint of Disney Book Group. No part of this book may be reproduced or transmitted in any form or by any means, electronic or mechanical, including photocopying, recording, or by any information storage and retrieval system, without written permission from the publisher. For information address Disney • Hyperion, 125 West End Avenue, New York, New York 10023.

First Edition, September 2018 • 10 9 8 7 6 5 4 3 2 1 • FAC-029191-18208 • Printed in Malaysia

This book is set in Macarons/Fontspring with hand-lettering by Ryan T. Higgins
Designed by Tyler Nevins
Illustrations were created using scans of treated clayboard for textures, graphite, ink, and Photoshop

Library of Congress Cataloging-in-Publication Data

Names: Higgins, Ryan T., author, illustrator.
Title: Santa Bruce / by Ryan T. Higgins.
Description: First edition. • Los Angeles ; New York : Disney-Hyperion, 2018.
  • Summary: Grumpy and cold when his forest friends insist he stay awake to
  celebrate Christmas, Bruce the bear, wearing his long underwear and warm
  hat, is mistaken for Santa by the youngest forest creatures.
Identifiers: LCCN 2018002680 • ISBN 9781484782903 (hardcover) • ISBN
  9781368026789 (ebook)
Subjects: • CYAC: Christmas—Fiction. • Bears—Fiction. • Forest
  animals—Fiction. • Santa Claus—Fiction. • Attitude
  (Psychology)—Fiction. • Humorous stories.
Classification: LCC PZ7.H534962 San 2018 • DDC [E]—dc23
LC record available at https://lccn.loc.gov/2018002680

Reinforced binding
Visit www.DisneyBooks.com

B ruce was a bear
who did not like the holidays.

He used to stay in bed all winter long
and skip right through the whole business.

But his family wanted
to enjoy a cozy, snow-filled
Christmas together.

So Bruce was awake.

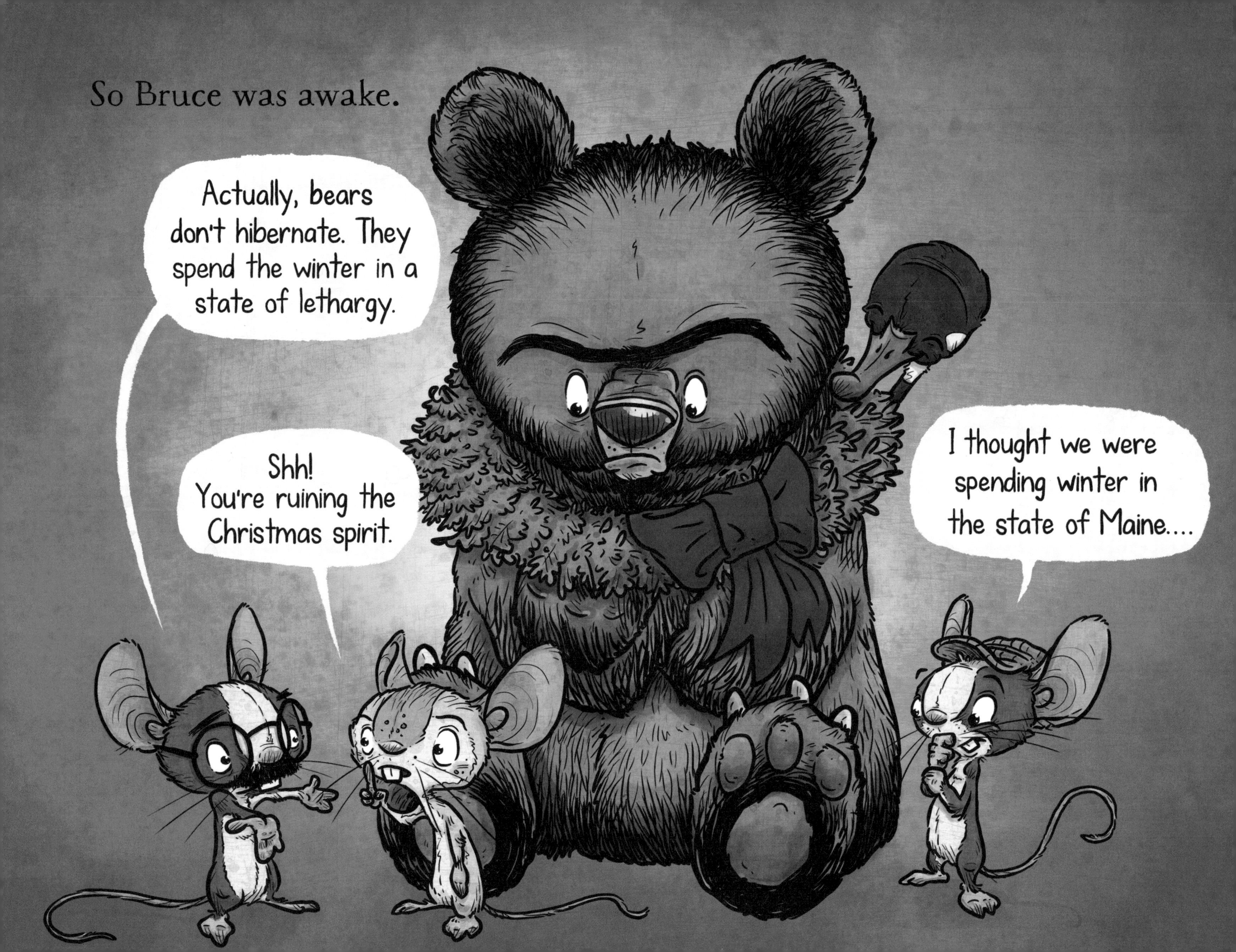

The geese had decked the halls.

The mice made lots of eggnog.

The holiday season was going to be filled with fun and cheer.

Bruce did not like fun.

Bruce did not like cheer.

Bruce did not like fun *or* cheer.

Bruce also did not like being cold.
Which is why he started wearing
long underwear and a warm hat.

And then it happened . . . again.

A case of mistaken identity.

Bruce did not like mistaken identities.

Bruce decided to ignore the problem
until it went away.

It did not.

It got worse.

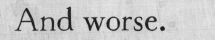

And worse.

SANTA!

Soon word spread,

I want ninety-nine red balloons for Christmas!

For Christmas, I want world peace.

and all the little critters of the forest wanted to visit Santa Bruce . . .

Finally, they all went home and
Bruce could grumble in peace and quiet.

But not for long . . .

KNOCK
KNOCK
KNOCK

. . . because all the parents wanted to thank Bruce for his Christmas spirit.

Bruce tried to tell them that he didn't have any.

Bah humbug!

That's when Thistle made an announcement.

Bruce wants to say you're welcome! AND what's more, Santa Bruce is going to deliver presents to all of your kids tonight!

And with that, the parents left,
shouting out with glee.

Bruce did not like glee.

Finally, Bruce headed to bed.
The mice had other ideas.

Bruce put his foot down.

But the mice were persistent.

The geese were helpful.

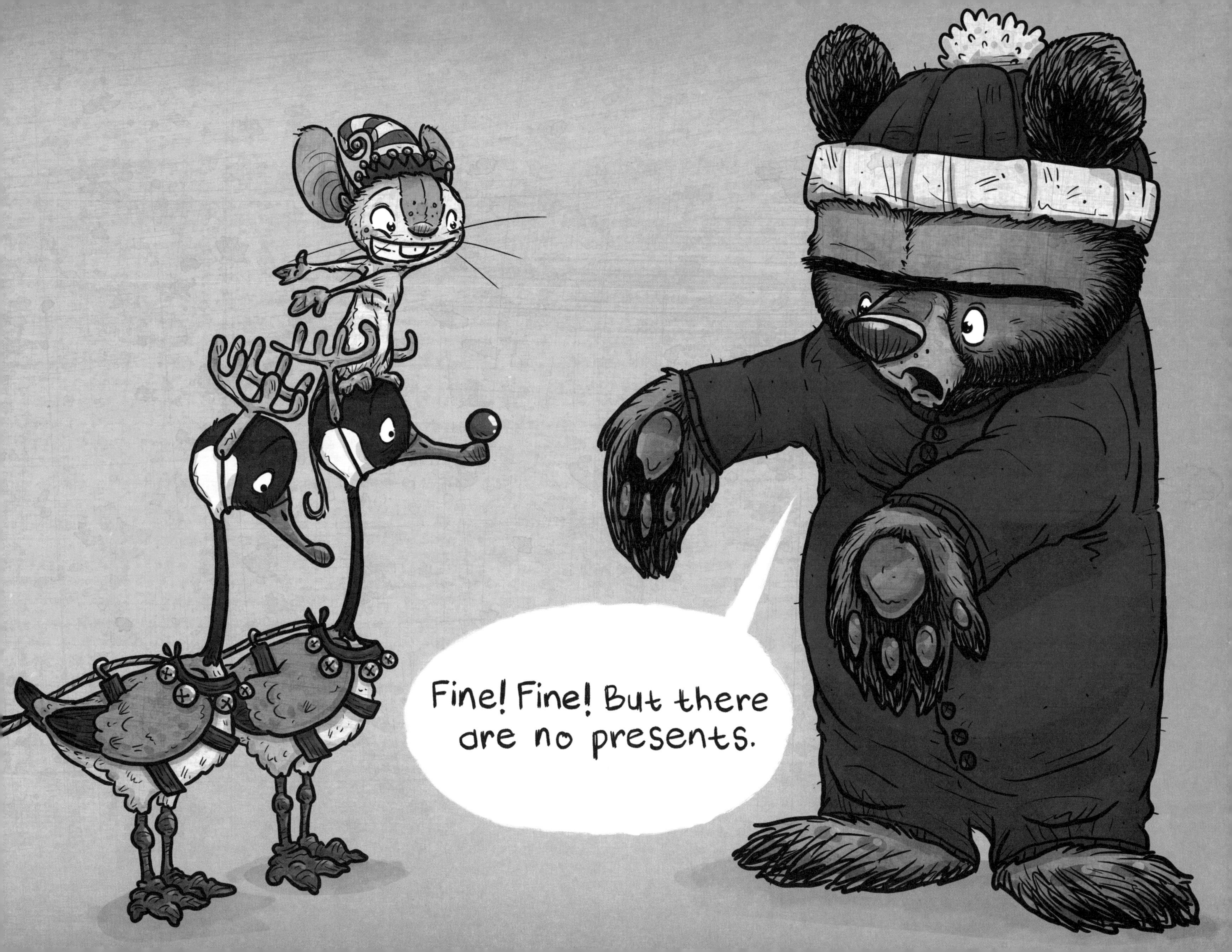
Fine! Fine! But there are no presents.

I'm still not going.
Pleeeeease?! All you have to do is sit in the sled.
We'll give you chocolate eggs....

Finally, the grumpy old bear agreed to be Santa Bruce for one night.

And everyone was very happy.

Being Santa Bruce
was not an easy job.

That is not a cookie.
That is soap.

And by the time Santa Bruce finally finished, the early morning light was creeping over a white Christmas.

Hollow Express

As all the critters of the forest awoke, they found presents waiting for them from Santa Bruce.

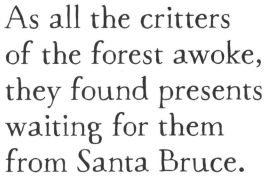

Bruce had spread the spirit of
Christmas all over the forest,
and brought everyone happiness.

MERRY CHRISTMAS,
BRUCE!!

Bruce did not like happiness.
He liked sleeping.

But Bruce's bed would have to wait.